state of the union

☙❧

state of the union

of the

union

A MARRIAGE IN TEN PARTS

NICK HORNBY

RIVERHEAD BOOKS • NEW YORK

RIVERHEAD BOOKS
An imprint of Penguin Random House LLC
penguinrandomhouse.com

Copyright © 2019 by Lower East Ltd.
Penguin supports copyright. Copyright fuels creativity, encourages
diverse voices, promotes free speech, and creates a vibrant culture. Thank you
for buying an authorized edition of this book and for complying with copyright
laws by not reproducing, scanning, or distributing any part of it in any form
without permission. You are supporting writers and allowing Penguin
to continue to publish books for every reader.

SundanceTV is a registered trademark and the SundanceTV logo
is a trademark of Sundance Enterprises, Inc.

ISBN 9780593087343 (trade paperback)
ISBN 9780593087350 (ebook)

Printed in the United States of America
1   3   5   7   9   10   8   6   4   2

Book design by Claire Vaccaro

This is a work of fiction. Names, characters, places, and incidents
either are the product of the author's imagination or are used fictitiously,
and any resemblance to actual persons, living or dead, businesses,
companies, events, or locales is entirely coincidental.

state of the union

❧

week one

∞

MARATHON

When Louise arrives, Tom is already halfway through a pint, and he's doing *The Guardian*'s cryptic crossword.

"Hey," says Louise.

"Oh," says Tom. "Hi. I bought you a drink."

"Thanks."

She picks it up and takes a sip.

"Thank you for coming," she says.

"Oh, that's okay."

"Have you been here long?"

"No, no," he says. "This is my fourth."

Louise looks alarmed.

"It's not really my fourth."

"Right. Phew."

She chuckles mirthlessly.

"It is my second, though."

"You're entitled to two," she says. "But won't you want a pee break?"

"I hope so. And I'll make it last as long as I can."

"But then it'll seem like you've been for a poo."

"Oh, hell. So then I'll announce right at the beginning that I can never poo in someone else's house."

Louise shows willing by making another noise intended to express amusement.

"I think I could say just about anything today and you'd laugh," Tom says. "Within reason."

"Well. Let's not test that theory out."

"Except what constitutes reason? There's a talking point."

"We've probably got enough talking points, without delving into the history of Western philosophy," Louise says.

"You're right. Who was the reason philosopher? I want to say Kant. I want to, and I will. Kant. There. I said it. Shall I check?"

He gets out his phone.

"Please don't. We've only got a few minutes."

"Sure? Won't take a second."

"I'm sure. But thank you. Were the kids okay? Did Christina remember she was staying late today?"

"All fine," Tom says. "Dylan got another detention."

"Oh, hell. What for this time?"

"He was doing an impression of someone I've never heard of in Geography."

"Idiot. Shall we talk about . . ."

"I mean, literally never heard of," Tom says. "A YouTuber, a grimy . . . Who knows? And Otis was feeling 'a little better' when I left. Surprise, surprise."

"Are you trying to fill the time before we go?"

"I suppose I am, a bit. I'm nervous."

"I'm sorry," Louise says. "If it wasn't for me, we wouldn't be here."

"No."

Louise looks at him.

"Just 'no'?"

"Yes. Just 'no.' If it wasn't for you, we wouldn't be here. A sad fact."

"You wouldn't take a tiny bit of the responsibility?"

"No," Tom says. "Why?"

"Because . . . Because it's a long and complicated road that has led us here. Don't you think?"

"Well. It depends which way you look at it. There's the long and complicated, and then there's . . . as the crow flies."

"Talk me through the route your crow flies," Louise says.

"You slept with someone else, and here we are."

Louise takes another sip of her drink and then a deep breath.

"But there's a bit more to it than that, isn't there?" she says.

"Which way do you go, then?"

"Crow or no crow?"

"Crow."

"Well. You stopped sleeping with me, I started sleeping with someone else."

"That's . . . That's a very short version. And quite crude, if you don't mind me saying so."

"See, my version is actually longer than yours," Louise says.

"Mine explains why we're here. Yours is a partial version of the long mess that came before."

Louise sighs and tries to gather her thoughts.

"Yes," she says. "I made a mistake. But . . ."

"Can I clear something up? How many mistakes was it in total?"

"Well. One."

"One."

"Yes. Depending on how you define it."

"Define it in the way that gives the highest number. Just so I know what we're dealing with."

"The highest number would be in the hundreds."

"Jesus Christ," Tom says.

"Because of all the tiny, tiny decisions that led to the big mistake."

"Oh. No. I'm not interested in the tiny decisions. We have to leave in five minutes."

"So one."

"But when you said, 'Depending on how you define it' . . ."

"You could define it as one affair," Louise says. "Or you could define it as four mistakes."

"How?"

"The original mistake repeated three times."

"I'm lost. How many times did you sleep with this guy?"

"Four."

"Not three, then."

"No. One mistake, three repetitions of the original mistake. The first time being the original sin, sort of thing. And the other three as duplicates."

"Four times. You can't write four times off as being accidental. You'd be hard pushed to write one off as accidental, to be honest."

He laughs at his own joke.

"I mean, how would that work?" he says.

"I told you. I had an affair. You're not consoled that it was only four times? Not forty?"

"Well, not really. Once you get to four, it might as well be forty."

"I think if it had been forty, we'd be having a different conversation."

"Yes. One with lots of forties in it. Instead of fours."

"You know what I mean," Louise says. "Forty would have meant it was going on for . . ."

She trails off.

"I'd like you to finish that sentence. How much time would it have taken you to get to forty?"

"This is a ridiculous conversation."

"I only wanted an approximate rate. So we can calculate frequency as well as number."

"Why?"

"Comparison."

7

"There is no comparison. It's like comparing a twenty-five-yard dash with a marathon."

"And we're the marathon?"

"Of course," Louise says. "We're married, with children."

"Except we didn't know that was going to happen when we started having sex. We weren't pacing ourselves. We didn't say, 'Best not go at it too hard or there'll be nothing left in fifteen years.'"

"Look. These four times took place over a few weeks. Our first four times took place over a few days."

Tom looks pleased.

"But where does that get us?" she says. "How long is it going to take us to get to four times from here?"

"What's 'here,' though?"

"Here. Now. When we're not having sex at all."

"Well. If you want to stick with the running analogy . . ."

"Which I'm not committed to . . ."

"At the moment," says Tom, "we're Usain Bolt with an injury. A groin strain, if you like."

"We're both Usain Bolt? Not just you?"

"Our sexual relationship is Usain Bolt with a groin strain. It's stalled. But once it starts up again, we'll get to four in no time."

Louise looks at her watch.

"We've got less than five minutes. We should sort out an agenda that doesn't involve Olympic runners."

"My agenda is, why did you sleep with someone else?"

"To answer that question, I suspect we have to answer a lot of others."

Tom sighs wearily.

"Really?"

He's distracted by something out the window.

"Look. They've just come out."

Another couple have emerged from the house across the street.

"You can see the house from here?"

"It's that one. With the green door," Tom says. "Those two. They've just been given a right counseling. They look shell-shocked."

"They're completely fucked."

"As in exhausted? Or as in no future for their relationship?"

"Both," Louise says. "Look. She's going to kill him."

The couple walk past the pub and disappear from view.

"Is that what we want?" Tom says. "To completely fuck our relationship? I mean, it's not as if there's nothing left of it."

"No, of course not."

"We've got two kids, for a start."

"Exactly. And . . ."

"Crosswords," says Tom hopefully. "*Game of Thrones*."

"Yes. When it's on."

"So do we really . . . I didn't know we were in a marriage that needed . . . poking round in."

"'Poking round in'?" says Louise.

"I suppose it's a medical metaphor."

"Well, it's a good one. If they opened you up and found you riddled with cancer, would you want them to sew you up again?"

"You know I don't like talking about cancer. Can't it be Ebola?"

"You'd rather have Ebola than cancer?"

"Ebola's harder to catch if you live in Kentish Town."

"Yes," says Louise. "But the whole point of the metaphor is that you've got it. Not that you haven't. If we'd managed to avoid all marital disease, we wouldn't be sitting here now."

"Fair enough. All right. Cancer."

"So would you like them to sew you up and pack you off?"

"I suppose it depends how far it had gone."

"Well, that's why they're poking round. They can't tell without a poke."

"Which is why I never go to the doctor's."

"Which takes us back where we started. You don't want to talk to anyone about our marriage. If it dies, you'd rather find out about it because it collapses on the spot."

"Exactly," says Tom. "You're a gerontologist. You know all about good deaths. Keeling over suddenly has got to be the best, right?"

"But that's a heart attack. Marriages never die suddenly. They've always been sick for a while before they kick the bucket."

"Oh, hell."

"I think what I'm saying, medically speaking, is that either we leave it and it kills us or we get it looked at."

She looks at her watch again.

"Okay?"

Tom nods, as if newly determined.

"Yes," he says. "I can't say I'm looking forward to it, but . . ."

"I don't want to run away from this," says Louise.

"No. Of course not. I mean, however badly it goes, it's only an hour."

"Oh. No. I meant the marriage, not the counseling."

"Oh. Hah."

"Before we go: Is it a man or a woman? You never said."

"I did," Louise says. "It's a woman."

"A woman? Oh, Christ."

"Wouldn't you have said the same thing if I'd told you it was a man?"

"Yes. Bad in a different way. If it were a man, I wouldn't be able to talk about anything intimate, obviously."

"Obviously."

"But if it's a woman . . . I'm going to get slaughtered."

"Slaughtered? Why won't she slaughter me?"

"Feminism."

Louise laughs disbelievingly.

"I know you had an affair," Tom says. "But it'll turn out to be my fault. Because of mitigating circumstances. Not just my . . . our . . . you know, the sex thing. But she'll find out you earn all the money and do most of the cooking even though you're at work and I'm not, and you do all the boring arranging stuff, and . . . I think she'll just

11

write you a blank check. Go on, Louise. Fill your boots, girl. You're entitled to ten affairs if you want them."

"I'm not sure marital counselors tell clients to have ten affairs. And I really don't want ten. The one I had was very stressful."

She stands up. Tom does likewise. They both drain their drinks.

"She's going to write it off, that's for sure."

"I won't let her. I'll tell her," says Louise. "I'll tell her exactly how bad I've been."

Tom gives her a look.

"I'm not sure we want the details, do we?"

"Not like that. I mean, how awful I was. How unfair and sneaky and . . . and morally reprehensible."

They leave the pub and cross the road. When they get to the other side, Tom stops.

"Let's walk up the road for a bit," Tom says. "Try to sort this out."

They start to walk away from the counselor's house.

"What are we sorting out?"

"Whether a man or a woman is best."

"It's a woman," says Louise. "Sitting there waiting for us. There's nothing to sort out."

"Well. Not necessarily. We could forget about this and look for a man."

"Who, as you point out, would be bad in a different way."

"I've changed my mind about that."

Louise is getting impatient.

"Come on, Tom," she says. "This was your idea in the first place."

She walks back toward the counselor's house. Tom follows. She rings the doorbell. They stand there, nervous. Suddenly, Tom runs away. He's running fast, as if for a bus.

"Tom!" Louise shouts. "TOM! Tom!"

But he ignores her and disappears from view.

week two

❦

ANTIQUE GLOBES

L ouise is in the pub on her own, nursing a glass of wine, sitting at the table where she and Tom sat a week ago. His pint is waiting for him. She is checking her phone when the couple who take the counseling spot before them emerge from the house. Louise watches through the window. All isn't well. The woman marches ahead while the man stands still and shouts at her. She keeps marching. Tom comes in, sits down, takes a sip of his drink, and watches with Louise for a moment.

"What have I missed?" Tom says.

"She's stormed off."

They watch as the man runs after her and grabs her by the arm. She takes a swing and catches him on the head, hard. He lets go of her arm and puts his hand to his face in disbelief. She marches on.

"Oh, for God's sakes. He's like a footballer," says Louise.

Over the road, the husband rubs his head and walks slowly and sadly in the same direction as his wife.

"She's just full-on walloped him," says Tom.

"Yes, but only up here. On the forehead. She'd have to be Mike Tyson to do him any proper damage."

Tom looks at her.

"What?" says Louise.

"I'd have thought you're anti–domestic violence. Of any kind."

"I didn't say I was pro-it. I said he was making a fuss."

"So if you thump me like that, how should I react?"

"You can say 'Ow,'" Louise says. "And express disappointment. But you can't roll around as if you've broken your skull."

"I note that you didn't say, 'I'd never thump you like that.'"

"I know you. You'd say, 'Yeah, okay. But what if you did thump me?' You'd push the hypothetical. That's what you do."

"Of course," says Tom. "But that doesn't mean you can just cut out the preliminary bit."

"That went without saying. I have never thumped you yet, and I never would."

"Ditto."

"There we are, then. Something to take in there and build on," she says. "How are you feeling about this week?"

"Well. I'm pretty sure I'll be there from the beginning."

"As opposed to fifteen minutes from the end."

"It took a lot of balls to turn up last week. And the later it got, the more balls it took."

"So if you turn up at the start this week, that shows . . ."

"Even bigger balls than turning up fifteen minutes from the end."

"Right," says Louise. "So there's basically nothing you can do that isn't an extreme act of heroism on your part."

"That's more or less it."

"You're so ballsy it's a wonder you can even walk. Must be like having two . . . antique globes down there."

"That was a bit sarcastic."

"Sarcasm's not allowed anymore?"

"Not considering the circumstances," Tom says.

"I can't remember the last time we didn't speak sarcastically to each other."

"Last week. In here. When you apologized and so on. I rather enjoyed it."

"So I'm not allowed to make jokes about your giant balls?"

"You were being sarcastic. About me not having giant balls. If I had giant balls and you were making jokes about them, well, fine. But you weren't. You were suggesting the opposite, really."

"Right. And I'm not allowed to, because I'm the one who's responsible for us being here."

"Exactly."

"Gotcha. Do you want me to tell you you have giant balls? I mean, sincerely? Is that where this is coming from?"

"No! Who wants giant balls?"

He looks at her suspiciously.

"It's not something you're interested in, is it?" he says.

19

"God, no."

"I wonder if anyone is."

"There's probably a website. There is for most things."

They both sip their drinks.

"So what's the agenda?" says Tom. "Not Lucy again."

"We got to the end of Lucy."

"I can't believe you even started on her."

"I was giving some context."

"I understand the relevance of Lucy's party. I just don't understand why you got into a twenty-minute conversation about Lucy."

"She wanted to know why you hadn't come with me on the night I, you know. Met Matthew," Louise says.

"I didn't come because I don't like Lucy."

"Yes, but why don't you?"

"Boring."

"The woman who has trekked through the Andes on her own?"

"That's the one. I never want to talk to anyone who's trekked through the Andes on their own ever again. They never shut up about it. Put some photos on Instagram if you must, but . . . Move on, woman! It's over!"

"Whereas someone who saw the Turds in 1989 is the most fascinating person who ever lived."

"That's the great thing about music. There isn't much to say, apart from 'I saw the Turds in 1989.' That's it. End of. Then you talk about someone else you saw back in the day."

"Kenyon was wondering if you felt a bit threatened by . . ."

Tom rolls his eyes.

"Will you stop making that face?" Louise says. "Her name's Kenyon. There's no point in disapproving of it."

"I don't disapprove of it. I just don't . . . believe it. It might be her surname, but I can't see that it's her first name."

"She said it was. Kenyon Long."

"That's two surnames."

"One of them's her first name."

"Well, I don't think so."

"You believe our marital counselor is lying to us about her name?"

"Who's called Kenyon? I mean, really?"

"She is. I can't see what advantage she's seeking by making it up."

Tom thinks about this for a moment.

"Maybe that's her counseling identity. Mild-mannered Julie by day. Nosy, judgmental Kenyon by night."

Louise sighs.

"Is there anything you want to talk about this week?"

"Not really."

"So let's move on to Matthew," she says.

Tom makes a face.

Silence.

"Really? I'd rather not."

"It's just that last week, you were of the opinion that there was no lead-up. I had an affair, and we decided to have counseling."

21

"Last week was last week. Counseling is an ongoing process. You discover things about yourself and the other person that you've never seen before."

Louise snorts.

"You've only done fifteen minutes."

"Perhaps all the more reason not to . . . leap in."

"So no Matthew."

"I don't think so," says Tom.

He doesn't offer up any alternative conversational topic. They sit there for a moment.

"Right. In which case . . ."

Silence again. They both look around the pub a bit helplessly.

The fighting couple walk into the pub. The man is upset, the woman regretful. She ushers him toward a seat and looks at him anxiously while she's waiting to be served. He starts to cry. Tom can't see him, but Louise can. She suddenly becomes more animated.

"What?" says Tom.

"He's crying."

Tom, too, is excited by the distraction. He starts to turn around.

"No! He'll see."

"Where is she?"

"She's buying him a drink."

"I just want a running commentary from now on," says Tom.

"We can't talk about our session?"

"No."

"She's given him his drink . . ."

"Brandy?"

"No. Just beer. And . . . she's not saying anything. She's just sitting there while he weeps."

"Oh, she's awful."

"It might be him. Supposing he's murdered one of their kids with an ax, and the full horror of it has only just dawned on him?"

"And she punched him because of the murder? Or because of the dawning?"

"But you know what I mean," Louise says. "Something like that, which would require counseling. The marital equivalent."

"An affair, maybe."

"An affair isn't the marital equivalent of murdering your child."

"Well, you would say that."

"Please, can we forget about them and get back to us?"

"I'm reluctant. They make us look good."

"We need to go, and we haven't agreed on where to begin."

She stands up, drains her drink, puts her coat on. Tom stays seated for a moment.

"We can't talk about Matthew because that's not the root cause. Not this week, anyway. Shall we talk about why we stopped making love?"

"Christ, no," Tom says.

"So we've got to go further back than that? How far back?"

"Oh, we've got loads. Your work. My work. Dylan's difficult spell.

23

Your mum dying . . . Bloody hell. When you think about it, it's like Brexit. There are going to be two years of talks before we even agree on what the issues are."

"Brexit is about divorce, though."

"That's the negative way of looking at it. What's happening behind me?"

Louise looks over. The woman is talking softly, in one long, unbroken stream, while the man stares unhappily ahead.

"She's talking to him."

"He's not speaking?"

"No."

"Well. There goes your child-murdering theory."

"Why?"

"Well, he didn't do the murdering, anyway. She's not saying, over and over again, 'You murdered our child.' No. She's had an affair."

"So why did she punch him?"

Tom thinks for a moment.

"I don't know."

"It's as if we hardly know them. Can we go back to Brexit?"

"If we must."

"It just is a divorce. I'm not being negative. Are you saying that's where we're headed? And will you stand up?"

He stands up, puts his jacket on, drains his glass.

"No. Of course not."

"Just checking: That's the last thing on your mind."

"Honestly?" he says.

"Honestly."

They walk toward the door.

"I don't know how it can be. Not when we're heading to see 'Kenyon.'"

He says the name satirically again.

They walk out into the street and toward the crossing.

"Is it the last thing on your mind?" says Tom.

"Yes."

"That's ridiculous. It's one of the ways this might play out. And the thing about Brexit . . . Some people believe that there are opportunities at times of great change."

"So you think you might be better off on your own?"

"God, no. I was talking about the country."

They cross the road.

"So what are the opportunities for great change that you're talking about?" Louise asks.

"Well. We won't get bogged down in all that red tape. We can do our own trade deals."

"I'm completely lost now. I don't want to talk about the country anymore. I'm trying to understand why a marital Brexit might be a great opportunity for you."

Tom shrugs. He's being shifty.

"Who are you going to do trade deals with? As far as I know, you weren't seeing any Italian or German women. I can't see that you'll have any more luck with the Chinese or the Americans. This is all rubbish."

They have arrived at Kenyon's front door.

"I'm just saying. It doesn't have to be the catastrophe that *The Guardian* thinks it is."

Louise stops dead and looks at him. He doesn't meet her eye. Tom raises his hand to ring the bell.

"You voted for bloody bastard Brexit. DO NOT TOUCH THAT DOORBELL. That's why you registered. Despite every single conversation we had."

"And it took giant balls, let me tell you. Because everyone I knew was banging on about what a disaster it would be."

"And that's why you did it? Because everyone else you know was doing something different?"

"It was part of the appeal, yes. I have some complicated but defensible socioeconomic views, too."

"Defend them."

"I'm not going to defend them outside 'Kenyon's' house a minute before marital therapy."

Louise rolls her eyes at the inverted commas.

"Defend one of them. A small one."

"Well, none of them are small. Believe me, I wish they were. But they're big. Big views. Big ideas. But mostly I wanted to annoy your friends."

"Oh, you've done that. They'll never speak to you again," Louise says.

"It's not something I want gossiped about. Like I said. It's a private matter."

"How will you annoy my friends if I don't tell them?"

"I was annoying them in the moment. While voting. I don't want to rub their faces in it. The nation needs to move on. Heal."

"Well, you can go and work in a care home for minimum wage. Replace all the East Europeans we've lost."

"I'm prepared to do my bit. Although I'm useless if there's any death involved. Or sickness. Or anything to do with the lavatory."

"But why didn't you just ask me . . ."

Tom rings the doorbell.

"Right," says Louise. "We're talking about Brexit. For the entire fifty minutes."

"Fine. How did Matthew vote?"

"How do you think?"

There is the sound of a buzzer, and they push on the door.

27

week three

❧

SYRIA

the pub is empty, apart from one man—the male half of the couple that goes in to see Kenyon before Tom and Louise. He is staring at the bar. His pint is untouched.

Tom walks into the pub, holding a newspaper. He goes up to the bar to buy himself a drink and sees the depressed man. Tom does a double take. The depressed man looks at him impassively. Tom nods a greeting. The girl behind the bar comes to serve Tom.

"A pint of London Pride, please. And a packet of dry-roasted." Tom watches the other man while his pint is being poured. He's desperate to say something. He opens his mouth and closes it again. He knows it wouldn't be appropriate to speak. He speaks.

"How's it going?"

The depressed man looks at him.

"Me?"

Tom is regretting his decision to ask.

"Sorry, I was just . . . It was more like a nod."

"A nod?" says the man witheringly.

"You know how you nod at people if you happen to be in the same place at the same time? Like that. 'How's it going?' That's all it was."

Tom nods exaggeratedly, and then tries again, with more modulation. The man looks at him as if he's a half-wit. The barmaid is back with Tom's pint and his nuts.

"Four pounds, please," she says.

Tom decides to try again with some conversation.

"Just getting a quick one in before the missus turns up," he says, and raises his eyebrows conspiratorially.

"What a brave lad," says the man.

Tom is wounded. He takes his pint and his nuts and sits down at their usual table. Louise comes in, sees him, and sits down. There is no drink in front of her.

"A glass of dry white, please," she says.

"Oh. Sorry. I forgot. I got flustered at the bar. Have you seen who's sitting there?"

Louise looks over.

"Ah. The battered husband."

Tom raises his eyebrows significantly.

"He's walked out."

"Gosh," says Louise.

"I can't buy you a drink, though."

"Why not?"

"I tried to talk to him, and it didn't go so well. I'm not going back up there."

"What on earth did you try to talk to him about?"

"I wasn't attempting a full-on conversation. I just nodded."

"Why?"

"I feel like I know him. It's an intimate thing, watching someone cry."

"And get smacked in the face by your wife."

"I nearly brought that up," Tom says.

"Why on earth would you do that?"

"Because . . . Well, he suggested that I wasn't being very manly."

"You gave him an unmanly nod?"

"That's the first conclusion you come to, isn't it? Not that he was being unreasonable. Not that he was being a macho prick. Oh, no. It has to be my unmanly nod."

"But what else could it have been, if all you did was nod?"

"I tried a . . . I don't know. A pleasantry. A nod with words."

"So an unmanly pleasantry, then? What was it?"

"Just, you know. 'Ooh, at last. A lovely pint.'"

"That seems quite manly."

"That's what I thought."

"Unless it was the 'ooh.' The 'ooh' could have sounded a bit, you know . . . effete."

"It wasn't an 'ooh.' It was more like . . ."

He gives a long, satisfied exhale, like a thirsty man being served a pint.

"No, that's all right."

"I thought so."

"And anyway," says Louise, "he's the crybaby."

"'Crybaby'? That's a bit harsh. You cried last week."

"I cried about Brexit, not about the terrible state of our relationship."

"Well. You didn't cry about Brexit per se. You cried about me voting for Brexit. So in a way you were crying about the terrible state of our relationship."

"The main reason I cried is because I work in the NHS and half my staff is European."

"Remember Kenyon said we weren't allowed to talk about it until we saw her today."

"And I also cried because you weren't honest about it."

"It's a private matter."

"Privacy and lying are different."

Tom makes a face suggesting this is a matter of debate.

"Anyway. Let's stop," he says. "Remember what Kenyon said. And I still think we're better off than those two."

"You can't be comparative about relationships like that. You can't look at a couple you don't even know and say, you know, 'Oh, at least we're not like them.'"

"I do."

"Your own happiness doesn't come into it?"

"Nope. Entirely dependent on other people being unhappier."

"You are absolutely not someone who jumps out of bed in the morning full of the joys of not living in Syria. You're miserable as hell. You have never once thought that you're better off than anyone."

Tom glances out the window of the pub.

"Here she comes."

The woman emerges from Kenyon's door.

"She's crying."

They look at each other. Even Louise is pleased.

"She's coming in here!" says Tom. "This is going to be good."

"Don't stare."

Tom stands up. He wants to get near the action, suddenly.

"Would you like a drink?"

"No. Sit down."

The woman walks into the pub. She goes up to her partner at the bar, pulls him off his stool by the hand, and takes him outside. Tom and Louise watch with rapt attention. Through the window of the pub, they see the woman say something to her partner. The depressed man looks at her . . . and then kisses her passionately. The kiss seems to go on and on, and the longer it lasts, the gloomier Tom and Louise get.

"Well," says Louise. "There goes Syria."

The couple break off, look at each other, and start kissing again.

"Can you imagine?" Tom says. "At their age?"

" 'At their age'? They're younger than us."

"Really?"

"They look it. Well, he does. Than you."

"Thanks. Anyway. That's still old enough to know better."

He looks at his watch.

"There's still time for your drink, if you want one."

"Hold on," Louise says. "This is important. 'Old enough to know better.' Can you explain? They're kissing."

"In public," says Tom with disdain.

"They are feeling passionate about each other."

"Well, if they feel that passionate about each other, what are they doing in counseling?"

Louise stares at him.

"What?" says Tom.

"Do you understand what you've just said?"

Tom thinks.

"I do now."

"It's not good, is it?"

"I can see why you say that."

"Are you suggesting there's no passion left?"

"Well. I don't see passion as . . . as petrol. Something that runs out. I see it as more like, I don't know, something you lose. Like keys." He picks up the pen he's using to do the crossword and waves it around. "Or this biro."

"Keys get found. Biros don't. So it's important for me to know which it is."

Tom doesn't say anything.

"Keys? Or a biro?"

Tom doesn't say anything. Louise is getting angry.

"Come on," she says. "Keys or a biro?"

"We seem to be in a position where if I say the word 'biro,' our marriage takes an ominous turn for the worse."

"So don't say 'biro.'"

"I hope keys. Of course. I'm working on the basis that it's keys."

"But either way, it's lost."

"Mislaid."

"Unless it's a pen."

"If it's keys, you look harder, don't you? That's why they get found. Pens get left all over the place. You might have left one under Matthew's bed."

"Was that necessary?"

"I'm just saying. If you'd left a ballpoint under Matthew's bed, you wouldn't necessarily have gone back for it."

"STOP! Enough. No more biros."

Tom puts the pen down. The couple outside start to walk up the road, hand in hand.

"Look," says Louise. "They've gone off for make-up sex."

"Won't solve their problems."

"Maybe not. But they're going to have a better evening than us."

"Maybe we'll have a breakthrough with Kenyon."

"The breakthrough would have to be a row," Louise says. "Row in there, make-up sex at home. We used to have good rows. And good make-up sex."

"Proper stand-up shouting matches," Tom says wistfully.

"Brexit was a row."

"We haven't made up, though. Could we have post-Brexit sex?"

"No. I voted in, and you voted out, and I hate you for it."

"We could come to an understanding."

"Oh, yes. Let's 'come to an understanding,' shake hands, and then fuck each other stupid."

"That's the thing. We were jogging along quite amicably until you started sleeping with someone else. I'll ignore that last bit."

"Why?"

"It was just . . . vulgarity for vulgarity's sake."

"Really? A lot of men would like to hear their wives use the phrase 'fuck each other stupid.'"

Tom looks around, anguished by the profanity, but Louise is in full flow.

"It suggests that there's still some life left somewhere," she says. "But not you. 'Jogging along.' 'Come to an understanding.' 'Amicably.' What is the point of being married? If there's no sex, no feeling, no passion, no nothing? You could have worn a T-shirt saying I VOTED OUT long before anyone ever thought of a referendum. Europe: You're out. Sex: You're out. Work: You're out. Marriage, life, friends: Out, out, out."

Tom looks at his watch.

"We should go," he says "We're late."

He stands up. Louise looks at him.

"That's it?"

"Well, yes," he says. "That's a reasonable summary of where I'm at. The work thing isn't by choice, but . . ."

Louise stands up. They walk out of the pub.

"You know what's wrong?" says Louise as they're waiting at the pedestrian crossing for the lights to change. "We've aged differently. I think forty is like thirty, except you have to go to the gym more. You think forty-four is like being sixty-five, except your children are younger. It's not over! Nothing is over! Where's your fight?"

She pushes him, quite hard.

"Ow," he says. "What do I need fight for?"

"'Do not go gentle into that good night.' It's not even night, for Christ's sake. It's not even teatime. Fight for your life. Fight for your marriage. Fight for work. Fight to be less bloody miserable."

The lights change. Tom walks ahead, embarrassed. The driver in the front of the traffic queue is watching them and laughing.

"Just . . . bloody FIGHT."

She pushes him again, in the back. He stumbles and falls. He breaks the fall with his arm.

"Oh, shit," says Louise.

Tom is lying on the ground, stunned.

"I think I may have broken my wrist," he says.

week four

&

PLASTER CAST

tom is sitting at the usual table by the window, a newspaper spread out in front of him. He's holding a pint in one hand; the other arm is wrapped in a plaster cast covered in signatures and little drawings. Louise comes into the pub. When she sees him she rolls her eyes. She walks over to the table and sits down.

"Really?" she says. "When there's nothing wrong with your arm?"

Tom doesn't say anything.

"Where did you get the cast from, anyway?"

"You can buy them online."

"And who signed it?"

"The kids."

"There are loads of signatures on there."

"Yeah. They were at it for ages. Making up names and practicing different autographs. It was actually quite a, you know, an educational exercise."

"You're a marvelous father. They'll be able to forge anything now.

So if you bought it online, it clearly wasn't a spur-of-the-moment decision."

"Next-day delivery."

"So you thought about it yesterday."

"Yeah," he says. "The day before yesterday, anyway."

"So two days ago, you were worrying about what to say to Kenyon about your arm."

"We told her I'd broken it! And I haven't broken it!"

"She'll be relieved to hear it."

"But we canceled the session because of it."

"Just tell her it was badly bruised."

"It is badly bruised," says Tom.

"So show her the bruising."

"It's internal."

Louise sighs.

"Kenyon must feel like the prime minister," she says. "There's a plan, and a goal, but she's firefighting all the time. You run away, you fall over, you pretend your arm is broken when it isn't . . . We never get anywhere near the actual marital problems. You know that I'm going to walk in there and tell her your cast is fake, don't you?"

Tom is aghast.

"What?"

"Why wouldn't I?"

"You'd grass me up?"

"You haven't been arrested. It's a marital therapy session. We go in there and tell the truth, otherwise what's the point?"

"We don't have to tell the truth about everything. What if I had, I dunno, an STD? Would you want to go in and talk about that?"

"Very much so, yes, seeing as I haven't given it to you."

"Yet."

"Charming."

"To be fair, I'm not the one who's slept with someone else."

"If I had given you an STD," says Louise, "then, yes, absolutely we should be talking about it. It would be a big deal."

"An STD is a bad example. What about if I'd hurt my penis in some way? Would you want to talk about that?"

"If you wanted to talk about it."

"I wouldn't."

"But what if you hadn't hurt your penis, but went in to see Kenyon pretending that you had?"

"Why would I do that?"

"Why would you put a fake cast on your arm? What's the difference?"

"Because I didn't tell her I'd broken my penis . . ."

"(You can't break your penis.)"

"(I am perfectly well aware of that.) I told her I'd broken my arm. I think this is a big moment for us."

"Explain?"

"You have to choose: Are you with me? Or are you with her?"

"I'm not going to play that game."

"It's not a game," Tom says. "Are we a couple? Two against the world? Or aren't we?"

"Two against the world?" says Louise scornfully.

"That's what marriage is, to me."

"You've just made that up. Because of the cast. Where do the kids fit in?"

"I'm against them, most of the time."

"Well, I'm not."

"So the four of us against the world, then."

"But that's family, not marriage."

"You know what I'm saying."

"I have never felt that it's the two of us against the world."

Tom holds out his hands as if she's just proved his point.

"Now we're getting somewhere," he says.

"What's the world ever done to us? We're hardly Romeo and Juliet."

"Go on. You're in a hole. Keep digging."

"How is it digging to say we're not Romeo and Juliet?"

"It's not very romantic."

"So in your fantasy, we're two lovestruck teenagers whose families don't want us to be together?"

"Obviously we're not teenagers. But there's the age gap."

"Four years."

"And the arts/sciences divide. That's a sort of modern Montague/Capulet thing. It's subtle, but it's there. A very faint whiff of, you know. Ooh, how does this work? Her a doctor, him a music critic?"

"First of all, no, it isn't there," Louise says. "And secondly, you need more than faint whiffs. The Montagues and the Capulets stabbed each other. They weren't whiffing faintly."

"Granted, there was no stabbing. But there was family pressure. My mum didn't want me to marry you."

"She warned me off."

"She warned *me* off."

"She told me I was much too good for you, you were bloody useless, and I'd end up leaving you," Louise says. "What did she say to you?"

"Yeah, exactly the same thing."

"That you were too good for me?"

"Ha, ha," says Tom mirthlessly. "Have you met my mother? No, of course not. The point is, I said to hell with her and married you anyway. Us against the world."

"Us against your mother, anyway. The rest of the world reacted with pleasure or complete indifference."

"Would you say honestly that you're on my team?"

"Yes. Of course I'm on your team. I support you, for a start. That's what you do with teams, isn't it?"

"That's a low blow."

"Saying you support someone is a low blow? I want you to do well. I worry about you. I . . . Well, I love you."

"'Well'? What's the 'well' doing here? What function does that serve?"

"I was just . . . I hesitated."

"Why?"

"People are allowed to hesitate. Hesitation is a thing."

"You hesitate when you don't know what you want to order in a restaurant. Not when you're telling somebody you love them."

"Love is a bigger deal than ordering a pizza, surely?" says Louise.

"If you're sixteen, yes. But not when you're married."

"You know why you hesitate when you're sixteen? Because you're scared you're going to look a fool. It's not because . . . well . . ."

"More welling. Well this, well that . . . 'Well' is fast becoming a very dangerous word."

"It's not because you have doubts."

"You have doubts?"

"Don't you?"

"No."

"That's a lie. How can you not have doubts? You don't want to sleep with me, we spend half the time arguing, you seem to be happier with other people than with me . . ."

Tom shrugs.

"I suppose my 'well' was supposed to indicate, you know . . . 'underneath it all,'" says Louise. "Underneath it all, I love you."

"Underneath it all."

"Yes."

"Great."

"To be honest, I think you should be happy with that. You're lucky there's anything still there."

"Let me ask you this: How would you feel if I left you for someone else?"

Louise thinks for a moment.

"Well," she says.

"'Well' again! Oh, that's great."

"You really don't like considered conversation, do you?"

"I notice you don't ask if I've met anyone."

"Have you met anyone?" says Louise wearily.

Tom doesn't say anything for a moment.

"Well," he says.

"Oh, very funny."

"Why can't I consider?"

"Because either you have or you haven't. And I don't think you have."

"There are all kinds of gray areas."

"Such as?"

"Online dating."

"You know you actually have to go out to do online dating, don't you?"

"No, you don't," he says. And then, less certainly: "Do you? I thought you did it online."

"You talk to someone online. And then you meet them. You haven't been anywhere that I know of."

"You don't know what I do during the day."

"But if you're going out to meet someone during the day, that wouldn't be a gray area, would it? You'd have met someone. Would you like to meet someone?"

"No. Not really. Where would that leave us? As a matter of interest?"

"Are you asking about an open marriage?"

"God, no," says Tom. "Unless that's what you want."

"No, it's not what I want. If you met someone you'd be moving out of this marriage and into a new relationship."

"What about you?"

"I suppose that's the fantasy, isn't it?"

"Is it?"

"Yes, when you've been married a few years and everything's . . . gone off a bit. You know it is," she says. "The fantasy is, you come home, your partner says he's met someone else and he's moving out."

"I don't suppose it's everyone's fantasy."

"Oh, it is, believe me. Is it yours?"

"Well."

"That'll do," says Louise.

"Can I leave my cast on?"

"Oh, what the hell."

"Thank you."

He looks at his watch.

"Shit," he says.

He drains his drink and stands up.

"We're late," says Louise.

She stands up, too, and they make for the door. Their path is blocked by Giles and Anna, former next-door neighbors who moved because of schools.

"Hello, you two," says Giles.

Tom and Louise are flustered.

"Oh. Hi," says Louise.

"How are you?" says Giles.

His eye falls on Tom's plaster cast.

"Oh, dear," he says.

"Oh. Yes," Tom says. "Bloody snowboards."

Louise looks at him.

"Oh, where have you been snowboarding?" Anna says.

"Well, all over, really."

"We haven't seen you for ages," says Anna.

"Stay for a drink," says Giles.

"We can't," says Louise.

"Not even a quickie?" Giles says.

"Afraid not," says Tom. "Another time."

"You're not going to the cinema, are you?" Anna says.

51

"Yes," says Tom gratefully.

"Ah, well, we're fine. We looked it up. Doesn't start for another twenty minutes. And that's the program, not the film."

"Useful to know," says Tom. "Very good reviews."

"You never know whether to trust them, though, do you?" says Giles.

"No. But I've got a good feeling about this one. One of Louise's colleagues was raving about it."

"We're not actually going to the cinema," says Louise.

"No. We're not," says Tom.

There's an awkward silence.

"Oh," says Giles. "How have you been, anyway?"

"Fine. Look, we've got an appointment," says Tom.

"We'd love to see you. Would you come round for supper? Or we could meet up for dinner halfway?" Anna says.

"Lovely," says Louise.

"There's lots to catch up on," says Anna.

"Great," says Louise.

She starts to push past them and into the street.

"I can see you're in a hurry, so . . ." Giles shrugs.

"We must seem very rude," Louise says. "There's a good reason for it."

"Marital therapy," Tom says. "You know what therapists are like if you're late."

"Oh, no!" says Anna, and she makes a sympathetic face. Tom tries to make the same face back.

"Afraid so," he says. "Spot of infidelity. Not me. Anyway."

He nods and goes out into the street. Louise, still inside the pub, stares at him as he walks past her.

Outside the pub, Louise is furious.

"What the HELL were you thinking of?"

"I'm sorry. I panicked. Didn't know how to break off the conversation."

"I cannot believe you just did that."

"No. Me neither."

"And throw that stupid bloody cast away."

Louise crosses the road without waiting for him. As Tom begins to follow her, he notices a rubbish bin. He stops, takes his plaster cast off, and puts it in the bin. He hovers for a moment, wondering whether he's done the right thing, and then scurries after her.

week five

❦

NORMAL SLOPE

om and Louise are sitting opposite each other in the pub, at their usual table, with their usual drinks. Louise looks at Tom searchingly.

"How are you?" she says.

Tom shrugs.

"Yes, okay. Did you remember my stuff?"

"Oh. Yes."

She reaches under the table and pulls garments out of her workbag. She puts a little pile on the table.

"Two pairs of socks, two pairs of pants, two T-shirts."

Tom looks at her aghast, and then glances around the pub.

"You didn't bring a bag?" he says.

"No. I was in a hurry. You called at eight-twenty this morning, which, as you may remember from when you were a part of the family, is quite a busy time. I ran to your drawers and shoved everything in my workbag."

"Now what do I do?"

"I'll put them back in my bag, and afterward we'll find a carrier bag."

She removes the pile and puts them back in her bag.

"Your top drawer, by the way, is pitiful," she says.

"What's wrong with it?"

"When was the last time you bought a pair of boxers?"

"I don't wear boxers."

Louise rolls her eyes.

"Or any underwear?" she says.

"I haven't worked for a year."

"So, thirteen months ago?"

"I can't remember."

"And you know you have access to a joint account. If I saw a payment to Marks and Spencer's for fifty quid, I'm not going to hit the roof."

"Fifty quid! Is that how much pants cost now?"

Louise sighs.

"No. I'm suggesting you buy several pairs."

"Can we change the subject? What have you said to the kids about me moving out?"

"Nothing."

"Nothing?"

"Not . . . as such," Louise says, choosing her words carefully.

"So what have they said to you?"

Louise shakes her head.

"It just hasn't been mentioned? I'm not there, and they haven't noticed?"

"If they ask, I just tell them you're somewhere else in the house. In bed. Listening to music in the spare room. In the pub."

"The pub? I never go to the pub."

"No, I know," says Louise. "But I think they like it. The dadness of it."

"Jesus. Wow."

"How long do you intend to be gone for?"

"I don't know."

"You don't have to do this. Nobody asked you to leave."

"We had a pretty terrible few days."

"And it all started with that stupid plaster cast."

"Well. I thought last week when you told her about throwing the cast away, you crossed a line."

"It was funny. She laughed."

"Yes," says Tom. "She laughed, you laughed. I was very hurt. I was making a gesture! Throwing the cast away was the first step on a very long road toward marital harmony!"

"Throwing a cast away when there's nothing wrong with your arm just takes us back to where you were. You're still a man with severe marital difficulties and two good arms."

"I wanted to show that I valued the truth."

"Is that why you told Giles and Anna there'd been a 'spot of infidelity' when we'd bumped into them over there?"

She nods toward the doorway.

"Yes. A spot. I was minimizing it. Another gesture," he says. "I admit I went over the top afterward, and then it all got a bit out of control."

"I'm sorry for some of the things I said."

"There were some low blows in there."

"Inevitable, I'd have thought," Louise says. "It's not your face I want to punch."

"I'd have thought you might want to encourage all body parts below the belt, not render them unusable."

"Yes, I'm sorry. But we should remember we're talking metaphorically. I didn't actually do anything to them."

"Metaphors in the nuts can hurt just as much as kicks."

"Is that really true?"

Tom shrugs, as if to say they'll have to agree to differ. They take sips of their drinks.

"It's a slippery slope, moving out," Louise says, "and it can be hard to climb back up it."

"I'd have thought that's the definition of a slippery slope."

"So you're saying you might not be able to get back up? You may have moved out for good?"

"Am I?"

"If you can't climb back up a slippery slope."

"I was merely pointing out a linguistic redundancy, not announcing the end of the marriage."

"So no slippery slope?"

"No," says Tom. "It's a normal slope, and I can wander up and down it at will. No slippage. Just exertion."

"To take account of the slope."

"Yes."

"Well, that's another thing. You're not as nimble as you once were."

"I just need a few days to think," Tom says.

"Where do you live, actually?"

"Why do you need to know?"

"I don't. Knowing where one's husband lives is just one of the useful pieces of information a wife may need."

"My mobile is on at all hours, in case of emergency."

"I'm not actually worried about how to get hold of you. I'm worried about what sort of state you're in."

"I'm perfectly comfortable."

"Please don't tell me you're at your mother's."

"No."

"Phew."

"That didn't work out."

"Oh, bloody hell, Tom."

"It was a bad idea."

"Who could have predicted that? So where are you?"

"I have a bed and access to a kettle, and that's all you need to know."

"Why won't you tell me?"

"Maybe there's not enough mystery in our relationship. That's what the advice columns are always going on about, isn't it?"

"I think they're talking about closing the door when you're peeing, not refusing to tell your long-term partner where you live."

"What are we going to tell Kenyon?"

"I'm surprised you want to tell her anything."

Tom looks relieved.

"Oh, thank you," he says. "I didn't think that would be an option. I owe you one."

"I was being sarcastic. Of course we're going to tell her that you've moved out of the family home since the last session. Bloody hell, Tom."

"Can we keep nothing private from that bloody woman? Do we have to do all our dirty washing in her launderette? Anyway, I don't want her to think she's not getting anywhere. It seems needlessly cruel."

"She'll live, I'm sure."

Louise takes a sip of wine.

"What do you need to think about?"

Tom looks baffled.

"How do you mean?"

"You said you needed a few days to think."

"Oh. Yeah."

"So tell me."

"Well. Everything, really."

"What is 'everything'?"

"The marriage," says Tom vaguely. "The, the . . ."

"So what have you thought in the two days you've had so far?"

"You're just putting me on the spot. What have you been thinking about?"

"I was asking you."

"I'm just pointing out that it's not that easy to come up with a list."

"I'm not the one who's gone off to think."

"I've been thinking a lot about your friend Matthew."

"Oh," says Louise cautiously. "What do you think about him?"

"Just that he's a bastard and I want to kill him. I think that, over and over again."

"And is that constructive?"

"Works for me. I googled him."

"How do you know his surname?"

"I saw an email."

"Oh."

"And then I googled and then I went on his Facebook page. He likes his beer, doesn't he?"

"No."

"His pies, then. I was surprised. He doesn't seem like your type. That England shirt he was wearing in his profile picture . . . looked like he had a football up it."

"Well . . . he isn't fat," she says. "And he wouldn't wear an England shirt. I think you may have the wrong person. Matthew is actually

63

quite serious-minded. I can't imagine him having a Facebook page, let alone an England shirt."

"Sounds like a lot of fun. Why did you stop? With him?"

"Because it was a terrible thing to do and it made me unhappy."

"And what if I don't move back in? Would it start up again?"

"I shouldn't think so."

"Why not?"

"This is a pointless line of questioning."

"Why?"

"Because . . . What are you asking me?" she says. "Really? What do you actually want to know?"

Tom thinks.

"I want to know if you'd start up with Matthew again. In the event of us splitting up."

"Yes, I know that. But what's the real question?"

Tom thinks, for even longer this time.

"Just . . . whether you'd see Matthew again. If we . . . stop being married."

"You're just saying the same thing over and over again."

"Because that's what I really want to know. Why wouldn't I want to know that?"

"All you need to know is that I'm not going to see Matthew again if we don't."

"God, you're brutal."

"Why is that brutal? I thought it might be consoling."

"Consoling? You're running off with Matthew the moment I'm out of the door and that's consoling?"

"Why would you care, if you're gone?"

"You see, that's the difference between us. I blame your job."

"What's my job got to do with it?"

"It's a brutal job," he says. "'Oh, I'm sorry, Mrs. Thompson, but you've got cancer, and as you're ninety, there's nothing we can do for you. Goodbye.'"

Louise looks at him incredulously.

"You honestly think that's what I do all day?"

Tom shrugs.

"You wouldn't know because you never ask," she says.

"Because I don't want to know. It's depressing. Who wants to look at old people's private parts all day? It's the worst job in the world. It depresses the hell out of me."

"I hardly ever look at their private parts. That's not normally what's wrong with them."

Louise pauses for a moment, and continues with increased volume.

"And anyway, they don't have that much bloody use for them. Because that's what happens. They shrivel up and become useless."

Tom looks around uncomfortably.

"It's happening to us now," she says. "As we speak. You know what the irony is? I work with old people, and you've spent your entire professional life writing about pop music. Thinking about young

65

people, in other words. Their gigs and their first albums and their drugs, and, I don't know, their groupies."

"Groupies? Have you ever read any of my stuff?"

"And I'm not sure what benefit it's had. You're shuffling around the house all day in your bathrobe. And I'm bringing you your clean pants."

"Make up your mind. What am I? Eight, or eighty?"

"There's room for confusion. But whatever it is, you're not forty-four. You're in the prime of your life. And what are you doing with it? You know what the real problem is with not having sex?"

"I can see it makes you crabby," he says.

"It makes you reevaluate everything. You live with someone, you have sex with them, you think, *Oh, I'm married to him.* Actually, you don't even think that. You don't think anything. You just get on with it. But take the sex away, and all you're doing is . . . sharing a house with some bloke who moans a lot and pokes fun at my bedtime reading habits. I mean, what's he even doing in bed with me?"

"I'm just trying to encourage you to branch out. There can't be that many Scandinavian women left to kill, surely?"

"Do you understand? Sex is the thing that separates you from everyone else in my life."

"Nearly everyone, anyway."

Louise stares at him coldly.

"We should go," she says.

They drain their drinks and leave.

"I'm sorry," says Tom as they wait at the lights to cross the road.

"Oh. Thank you. Me too."

"I didn't know it was that important to you."

"Really?"

"Look. How about I come back after the therapy session, and we can, you know. Have a bash, if you want."

The lights change. They cross the road. Louise doesn't say anything.

"Probably didn't say that very well," says Tom.

"No. When you say, 'Have a bash, if you want' . . ."

"Yes. Awful."

"Well, I don't. Want."

"Oh. Right. So . . . Where are we?"

"I don't know, Tom. But unless someone makes some kind of effort . . ."

"And by 'someone' you mean me, I suppose?"

She rings the bell by the therapist's door without answering his question.

week six

✺

NIGEL AND NAOMI

L ouise gets to the pub first. She buys the drinks and heads to their normal table in the pub. Tom walks through the door. He's wearing a sport jacket and a shirt. He has shaved and had a haircut. Before he notices Louise, he pats his hair nervously.

They both sit down, and he gives her a smile.

"Hi," he says.

Louise makes a little face, as if a smile and a "Hi" are weird. And she's right—they are, in the context of the normal dynamic between them.

"Hello," she says.

"How's your day been?"

"Oh, you know."

Tom leans in and makes eye contact.

"No. Tell me."

Louise is perturbed.

"What?"

"Nothing," Tom says. "I was just waiting for an answer to my question."

"There's nothing weird about me?"

"No. You look nice."

"Oh, I see. Please stop now."

"Stop saying you look nice?"

"All of it. The looking at me. The smiling. The . . . getup."

"It's not a 'getup.' I'm not wearing fancy dress."

"The effect is somewhat similar," she says.

"I'm trying."

"I can see that. Try in a different way."

"Give me some tips."

"For example, the text you sent me this morning . . ."

"Ah," says Tom. "More things like that?"

"No. Nothing like that."

"What was wrong with it?"

"It was creepy."

"'Looking forward to seeing you later'? That one? That's creepy?"

"Yes."

"Jesus."

"It sounds like you're trying."

"I am trying."

"Well . . . Don't."

"I'd try if you were someone new."

"Of course. But I'm not. Were you actually looking forward to seeing me?"

"Yes."

"I don't believe you," she says.

"Weren't you looking forward to seeing me, then?"

"I saw you yesterday."

"But that was just parenting. We haven't had a chance to chat."

"A catch-up?" Louise says sarcastically.

"If you want."

"It's not really starting again, though, is it? You catch up with people you've known for a long time. If we stay living apart, then that's what we'll be doing in the future. 'How have you been?' 'The kids are doing well, aren't they?' 'Have you got any good graduation photos?' 'Nice to meet you, Naomi.'"

"Who's Naomi?"

"Or Jenny, or Jackie. Or whatever. Your new partner."

"And that doesn't make you feel a little bit sick?"

"No, not really. I mean, if we do split, I'd like us all to get on."

"'Us all' includes your new partner, I presume. Russell or Nigel or Colin."

"Oh, thanks a bunch."

"They were just examples of names."

"Really crap names."

"They might be nice people. You wouldn't turn your nose up at Russell Crowe. Or Colin Firth. Or Nigel . . . Kennedy."

"Nigel Kennedy?"

"Nigel . . . de Jong, then."

"Who's he?"

"The Dutch player who should have been sent off in the World Cup Final. Studded a Spanish player in the chest. Right up here."

He points to his own chest.

"Terrible challenge, it was."

"You're not selling him to me," says Louise.

"I'm sure he's not like that at home."

"Anyway, you weren't thinking about those people. You were thinking about home counties bank managers."

"Nothing wrong with home counties bank managers. We could do with one in the family. And as my solvency is a problem, I don't think you should be too sniffy."

"Can we not talk about my next partner?"

"Let's talk about mine, then. What does Naomi do, as a matter of interest?"

"Naomi . . . Hmmmm. I'm not getting anything."

"Well, choose me someone else, then. Jenny. What does Jenny do?"

"She's just opened her own coffee shop."

Tom makes a face, like, *Not bad. I can see that.*

"You went in there to work every day, and got to know her, and . . . the rest is history."

"Well, history in the future, anyway. Speculative history. A new literary genre."

"Oh, and she loves kids, but she missed her moment because she spent too long with a guy who couldn't make up his mind, and now it's too late."

"Why is it too late?"

"Because she's too old."

Tom shakes his head.

"You're not palming me off with Old Jenny."

"You're well into your fifth decade."

"Jenny isn't."

Louise laughs.

"Older men are always going off with younger women," says Tom. "Rod Stewart. Mick Jagger. Rupert Murdoch. Nelson Mandela."

"And what have they got that you haven't?"

They are enjoying this conversation. They are amused and animated.

"It's more what I've got that they haven't. I'm younger than any of them."

Louise looks at him.

"I'd say you're drifting into unwise territory here."

"Yes, I can see that."

"I mean, if you do have children, although that might be . . . Anyway, if you do, you'd be good for a game of football in the back garden. But as for the rest of it . . ."

"I'd probably be better at IT stuff than Rupert Murdoch. He wouldn't know what to do with Spotify."

"He'd have staff."

"He wouldn't be allowed to use them in a contest."

"Fair enough."

"Plus, I'd kill Murdoch at tennis. I've got a height advantage, as well as an age advantage."

"You should challenge him. Settle this once and for all. If you explained that you needed to beat him to show that you're entitled to a younger second wife, I'm sure he'd oblige."

"I could ask if he's heard of Stormzy at the same time. Just to twist the knife."

"Oh, he'd know all about Stormzy."

"How?"

"Kids. A much younger wife. Several tabloid newspapers and a few TV channels."

"Again, he wouldn't be allowed to consult. I wonder whether we're drifting away from the matter at hand."

"Which is?"

"Well," Tom says. "Perhaps we should be talking about this marriage, rather than future marriages. Or Rupert Murdoch."

"It seems to me that the further we drift, the happier we get."

"Weird, isn't it?"

"Well. Not really. A malfunctioning marriage is depressing and time-consuming. Imagining a future with Jenny from the tea shop and Nigel from the bank is quite liberating."

"But you can always do that. Imagine a future that's easier than the one you have now."

"Is it as much fun living on your own as you thought it would be?" she asks him.

"I never thought it would be."

"Of course you did. Everyone does. Every adult who has children and a spouse imagines an empty flat, no clutter, a white rug without Coke stains all over it, a big double bed to oneself, a remote control without tape wrapped round it, drawers that weren't full of crap . . ."

"We could have a go at the drawers . . ."

". . . A toilet that isn't streaked yellow or brown because nobody ever puts the seat up or uses a brush, a hallway that isn't full of discarded trainers and bikes that nobody can be bothered to fix, doors you can lock because the keys are in the door, fart-free air, and, in the unlikely event that I did pass wind, I would not then greet my indiscretion with howls of laughter. Oh, quiet. I'd like to live somewhere quiet, with no hip-hop coming from the bathroom, nobody screaming at an Xbox . . ."

"I've stopped doing that now I'm better at Call of Duty, so . . ."

"Nobody complaining about the quality of the Wi-Fi, as if somehow I had authorized a cheap version, no cat puke to clear up . . ."

Tom's attention is distracted by something he's seen out the window.

"Ay, ay. A new couple."

77

A man and a woman in their seventies are emerging from Kenyon's house.

"Jesus," Louise says. "Why bother? If we're still having troubles when we're that age . . . Well, we won't be. I'll be long gone."

"Maybe that's the time to do it."

"Why?"

"Well. Dying alone and all that. The stakes are high."

"You think about that?"

"I'm living in a squat with three media studies students," Tom says. "Of course I think about dying alone."

"You never told me it was a squat! Oh, Tom."

"Can we talk about that another time? I think this is important. You must see people who are going to die alone all the time."

"They're going to die in a hospital, most of them. Surrounded by lovely Polish nurses. You're not even going to have that."

"Why not?"

"Because you voted to chuck all the Polish nurses out," says Louise. "Why is it all about you dying alone? Not me?"

"You don't seem to be bothered. Anyway, it's not really the dying bit, is it? It's the year or two before."

Louise picks up her glass.

"Here's to a heart attack."

Tom returns the gesture.

"Or a road accident."

"Did you ever have a baby pact with anyone?"

"I'm not sure," Tom says cautiously.

"I had one with Neil. When we were both single. We agreed that if we weren't with anyone by the age of thirty-five, he was going to impregnate me."

"The normal way?"

"Yes, the normal way."

"Neil Parker? Your old college friend?"

"Yes, Neil Parker."

"You were going to have sex with Neil Parker?"

"To get pregnant."

"So this is another one. Fucking hell."

"No! That's the whole point! It's a last resort!"

"Christ," Tom says gloomily. "Neil bloody Parker."

"Look, forget the sex part. The point is that we make a death pact instead of a baby pact. If it looks like we're going to die alone, we move in together. Or move into the same retirement home. Or something."

"Great. At least this week we can take something positive to the session. A death pact."

"I think it's positive. It shows a certain goodwill."

"It wasn't what I was hoping for when I bought a new shirt and got myself a haircut."

"What were you hoping for?"

Tom shrugs helplessly. Louise looks at her watch, drains her drink, stands up. Tom follows her lead.

"How are new starts possible?" Louise says. "When you've been together for a long time, and you have kids, and you've spent years and years being irritated by the other person? But if they stop being irritating, they're not them anymore."

"My text was me not being me."

"Exactly."

They walk to the door.

"So I've got to stay as me."

"Yes."

"While at the same time being different, somehow."

"It's a conundrum."

They walk to the crossing point.

"Can I ask you something?" says Tom.

"Of course."

"Jenny's coffee shop . . . Is it doing okay, do you think?"

He's being serious. He wants to know. Louise takes it seriously.

"Early days, but promising signs," she says. "A lot of mums from the local primary school are starting to use it, and they're spreading the word."

"So I'll probably have to find somewhere else to work?"

"Maybe."

"Nigel doesn't have to be a bank manager, you know."

"Good. That's the most generous thing you've ever said to me."

They have reached the front door. Louise rings the bell, and the moment of harmony is preserved.

week seven

❧

CALL THE MIDWIFE

tom is sitting with his pint, at the usual table, doing a crossword. Louise's drink is waiting for her. The crossword has been printed off—it's on a piece of A4 paper—and some parts of it are damp from the pub table. He's finding it difficult to fill in one of the clues, and he swears to himself.

"Fucking thing."

Louise enters the pub, walks over, sits down, and takes a big glug of white wine.

"Ah, that's better."

No response. She exhales exhaustedly. Everything indicates that she has had a difficult day, but Tom won't pick up on the cues.

Louise nods at the crossword.

"Who's the setter today?" she says.

"Arachne."

"Looks like you're getting on okay."

"Not too bad. Except I hate doing the crossword on a bloody piece of paper. It's either wet or bumpy."

"Why have you printed it off? Why aren't you doing it in the newspaper?"

"Because you've got the newspaper."

"Are you serious?"

"You know you have."

"Why won't you buy another newspaper?"

"You know it's two quid now, don't you? So that would be four quid a day."

"But it's not four quid a day, because we're separate people. We don't live together. You might as well add up all the money your friends spend on *The Guardian*, and say it's fifty quid a day."

"Six, more like," Tom says gloomily.

"Oh, for God's sakes. You've got hundreds of friends. Lots of friends, anyway. But we're getting off the point. You can afford to buy a paper."

"It seems like a big step."

"It's really not."

"Like I've committed to leave my home."

"How about this? If you move back in, don't buy a second paper."

"Jesus. I was only talking about the crossword, and we're back here again. Don't you get tired of our marriage?"

"Yes! Yes! Tired! Bored out of my skull! But how can we stop, if

84

you sit here complaining about how you can't afford to buy a news-paper?"

"I wasn't complaining. I just said it was a step I wasn't prepared to make."

"A symbolic step?"

"If you like."

"No. I don't like. I'd rather you just bought the paper," Louise says. "The point I'm making is that from the moment I walked in, you've been talking about our marriage, through the medium of the crossword."

"Just by saying I didn't like doing it on A4?"

"Have you never heard of subtext?"

"You're reading too much into it. As my mum used to say when I tried to talk to her about Bob Dylan."

"And was she right or wrong?"

"She was wrong then, I'm right now. Sometimes a crossword is just a crossword. And I can't write properly when the paper gets wet."

"The conversation could have gone an entirely different way."

"For instance?"

"You could have not mentioned the wet paper," Louise says.

"Well, obviously I wouldn't have done if I'd known that complain-ing about wet paper—and the little bumpy bits on the table . . ."

"Oh, believe me, I know it's not a frivolous complaint . . ."

"If I'd known that complaining about wet paper . . ."

"And the bumpy bits . . ."

"Was going to be the opening scene in a Bergman film."

"Let's start again."

To Tom's bemusement, Louise stands up and walks out of the pub. He waits for a moment, but she doesn't come back immediately. He starts to look at the crossword, and is no longer looking at the door when Louise walks in and sits down. She picks up her wine, takes another large swig.

"I needed that."

Tom smiles vacantly. Louise exhales ostentatiously. Tom suddenly spots an answer, tries to write it in, and is immediately frustrated by the scratchiness of the biro on the stains and the table.

"Fucking thing."

"Jesus Christ."

"Have I gone wrong already?" Tom says.

"Yes!"

"How?"

"I wanted you to ask me what sort of day I'd had."

"How was I supposed to know that?"

"So, first of all, it's often a conversation starter, isn't it? Between partners? 'Hi. How was your day?'"

"Gotcha."

"And secondly, I gave you all these cues. I took a swig of my wine, and then I exhaled, and . . . well. Never mind. Your way gets us back to the dual-newspaper problem within two seconds."

She shakes her head.

"What sort of day have you had?" Tom says.

"It's too late now. Have you noticed that we only ever seem to be able to talk about the last few seconds?"

"That's not true."

"We start talking, somebody says the wrong thing, and then we spend the rest of the time talking about the wrong thing someone has said."

"Yeah. That's what happens in counseling every week."

"Exactly. We come out in exactly the place we went in."

"Or a little further back, usually."

"What happened last week?" says Louise.

"I can't remember. We'd had that conversation in here about the names of our new partners, which we rather enjoyed . . ."

"She asked us how the week had been . . ."

"She always does that . . ."

"Then what?"

"Did we have an argument about the cost of the cat's medication? Or was that the week before?"

"The week before," says Louise. "Got it! *Call the Midwife*."

"Oh, yes."

"It didn't get us very far, did it?"

"I thought it was useful."

"In what way?"

"Because she interrupted you a couple of times to let me finish.

You've never let me finish before. So we learned the value of counseling and safe spaces."

"I only interrupt when you're talking about *Call the Midwife*. And that's because there is no end to your loathing. You know I enjoy it. I find it relaxing."

"Well, you shouldn't."

Louise laughs in disbelief.

"I shouldn't?"

"No. Why can't you find Preston Sturges films relaxing?"

"Which one is he?"

"*Sullivan's Travels*," Tom says impatiently.

"Can I make a confession?"

"Within reason."

"I don't really like black-and-white movies. I mean, I can see they're good, some of them. But . . . there's something about them that feels a bit like eating your greens."

Tom is stunned.

"*Double Indemnity*?"

"Yes."

"*The Maltese Falcon*?"

"Yes."

Tom thinks.

"*Jules et Jim*?"

"Yes!"

Tom is still thinking.

"I'm worried that you're going to name every black-and-white film ever made, and I'm going to say yes to all of them."

"Oh my God," says Tom. "I really had no idea."

"I'm sorry. I'm just . . . I'm not a critic. I like what I like."

"'I like what I like.' I never thought I'd end up with somebody who could say that and mean it."

He shakes his head.

"The trouble is, marriage is like a computer. You can take it apart to see what's in there, but then you're left with a million pieces."

Louise sighs in despairing agreement, and then rallies.

"How about this?" she says. "We shove the big bits back in, chuck the small ones away, close it up, and get on with things."

"But it won't work."

"It won't work, but it will look like a computer."

"Is that what you want? A marriage that looks like a marriage? Even though it won't work?"

"Well, it would be a start. At the moment I have a husband who won't sleep with me and lives somewhere else entirely. I might as well tell everyone I'm married to Brad Pitt."

"Yeah, well, good luck getting him to watch *Call the Midwife*."

"He doesn't have to watch it. He just has to not go on about how much he hates it."

"I had to watch it."

"Once. And only because you kept slagging it off without having seen it."

89

"So he's got to watch it once."

"And I'm sure if he does he'll respect my enjoyment and not make puking noises all the way through."

"We're getting sidetracked again."

"Let's do a couple of crossword clues before we go in. A morale-boosting exercise."

She moves her chair so she can sit next to him.

"Oh, look," she says. "Twenty-seven across. 'Game of cricket put strain on marriage.' Test match."

"Quite an easy one. Hadn't noticed it."

"Remember we're team-building, not point-scoring. Sixteen across. 'Party touring Russian capital to shared bed.'"

"Are you deliberately picking out the clues about marriage?"

"No! And 'shared bed' doesn't mean marriage. As we know. But do another one. One across. We need that. 'Rogue caught mate dividing loot.' Ignore the word 'mate.'"

"I can't," Tom says. "It's a crossword."

"Begins with *s* and ends in *g*."

"So 'loot' is 'swag' . . ."

"*Scallywag*. 'Ally in swag.'"

"With the *c* from 'caught.' There we are. Morale boosted. Team rebuilt."

Louise takes the pen and writes in the word.

"Oh. It's all wet and bumpy. That's annoying."

Tom gives her a look.

"Let's actually make a plan for this evening's session," she says. "Let's not go in and start arguing about something completely bloody irrelevant. Go in with an agenda. What are the big pieces we want to shove back into the computer? I don't even know if computers have big pieces, do they?"

"They must do. Batteries, and . . . valves. Not microchips. They're small. I might take that dead one apart tomorrow. I can take it back with me when I've had dinner with the kids."

"Would that be a good use of your time?"

"As good as anything else."

"I so hate you having nothing to do."

"Thank you."

"I mean . . . I am being sympathetic. But it's embarrassing, too."

"Oh."

"And it drags us both down. Sorry. But if we don't tell it straight, what's the point? You haven't started this biography yet?"

"Still researching. I think I may have to go to Cape Verde."

"Is that where your guy came from? What's his name?"

"Horace Silver."

"I thought you'd decided on someone else in the end."

"It turned out not to be the end."

"So Horace came from Cape Verde."

"No. His dad."

"You're going to Cape Verde because that's where his dad was born? How many copies is this book going to sell?"

"Oh, nowhere near enough to cover the cost of the flight. So . . . Yeah, expensive and pointless. I probably won't go. Probably won't even write the book. I don't know why I say all this crap."

"To give yourself hope. That's understandable."

"I'm not sure there is much hope. The world has changed. Nobody wants music writers anymore. There's no paid work. Time has moved on. I'm like a coal miner, or a blacksmith. Is it embarrassing, living with an unemployed blacksmith?"

"It's not your fault."

"Well, it sort of is. I got a degree in English, but I couldn't be an English teacher or an English tutor, could I? No. Not good enough for me. I had to chase after the free drugs and the expenses-paid trips to L.A."

"Yes. Inexplicable."

"I should have thought things through."

"You couldn't see the Internet coming. Just like blacksmiths couldn't see cars coming."

"Oh, they should have seen cars coming," says Tom. "It was only a matter of time."

"So you're saying you're smarter than a blacksmith?"

"Not as such. But I'd like to think that if my dad had been a blacksmith, and he was trying to hand over the keys to the shop, I'd have said, 'No, Dad. Those days are coming to an end.'"

"Right. And what would you have done instead?"

"I don't know. Advertising. PR. What year are we in? And what part of the country?"

"Oh, I'd have moved."

"If you manage to prove to me that you're smarter than a blacksmith, how far down the road toward marital harmony will it get us?"

"I was just defending myself."

"No, you weren't. You were attacking blacksmiths for their bad choices."

"I have to take pleasure where I can find it. Attacking blacksmiths is about all I've got left."

Louise sighs.

"Are you thinking that we should give Kenyon up?"

"Yes. Yes. Of course. Every week. Are you? We're going backward. As you said."

Tom notices the elderly couple leaving Kenyon's house. The man is walking with particular difficulty. He has to stop halfway across the road.

"He's not getting any quicker, is he?" he says.

"She's a marital therapist, not a personal fitness guru."

They watch as the old couple come into the pub. Louise and Tom watch them intently—rudely, even. The woman points to an empty table nearby and the man shuffles off to sit at it. The elderly woman turns to them and smiles.

"How are you getting on?" she says.

Tom is aghast.

"What?"

"With Kenyon," the woman says. "We couldn't help but notice you knocking on the door last week."

"Wow," says Tom. "That's a bit . . . It is supposed to be private, you know."

Louise smiles.

"We've watched you coming out," she says.

"Speak for yourself," says Tom to Louise. "I'm not interested in other people's personal business."

"We think she's very good," says the woman. "We've been seeing her on and off for years. It takes time, that's all. You've got to get through all the hurt and the petty niggles. But you're young. You've got lots of time. Lucky you. Anyway. Good luck."

She crosses her fingers for them and goes to the bar. Tom watches her go. Louise gathers her things and stands up.

"That was rather sweet, didn't you think?" says Louise outside the pub. "Like a film. An elderly woman gives a younger couple good advice, and saves their marriage."

"That's a color film, if ever I saw one. Anyway. Did you hear what she said? Years and years. Hurt and niggles."

"But maybe we can do it quicker," says Louise.

"Not at the rate we're going. Not with *Call the Midwife* and A4 paper and so on. We'll be in there fifty years."

"So let's get down to it."

"What does that mean?"

"Let's give it to each other straight."

"No more subtext?"

"No more subtext."

Tom makes a show of rolling up his sleeves.

"Okay, then," he says. "Bring it on."

week eight

❦

DOLPHINS

om is at the bar, buying the usual round. Louise is sitting on the sofa in the pub, because their normal table is occupied. Tom hasn't seen her, and she's got a glass of white wine and a pint of bitter already. She's looking good. She's wearing lipstick and a plunging sweater—she's the one making the effort. As Tom picks up his drinks and walks toward their usual table, she gestures at him. He comes over and sits down, puts Louise's second glass of wine down.

"Oh, well."

"Not to worry. Don't have to drink them both."

"Hello," she says sweetly.

"Hi."

He looks at her. She gives another smile.

"You haven't started . . . You're not going out on a date afterward, are you?"

"No!" says Louise. "I just thought . . . After last week's session . . ."

"Which bit?"

"When you told me I was unsexy."

"I didn't say that."

"You did. I listened to it again to check."

"What? How?"

"I've been recording the sessions."

"Seriously? You record the sessions and listen again?"

"Yes," she says. "I put my phone on the coffee table before the second session and Kenyon asked if you were okay with it and you said yes."

"Oh. I see. I thought she was asking if I was okay with you putting the phone on the coffee table."

"That would have been weird."

"Not as weird as recording the sessions. When do you listen?"

"They're good for dog walking. They're pretty gripping, actually."

"Like a BBC radio drama sort of thing?"

"Yeah. Except there are some credibility gaps. Like, wow, these two people would never get together in real life."

"That's the beauty of real life, though, isn't it? We did get together."

"Yes, I noticed that much. And we are where we are. My point was that it might not have been a good idea."

"Not . . . on paper. But the real world is gloriously unpredictable. And here we are, with two wonderful children. Are you wishing them away?"

"Of course I'm not," Louise says. "But maybe we should have had two wonderful children with other people."

"So four wonderful children? Who wouldn't even know each other? The thought of that breaks my heart."

"Why would you even care whether they know each other or not?"

"Because they'd be . . . They'd be half brothers, kind of."

Louise laughs in disbelief.

"They might not all be boys. And they would absolutely not be related."

"I think they would be. Spiritually."

"So do you think ours are related to what's-her-name's children? Your ex? Sinead?"

"No, of course not."

"But you could have had children with her."

"That was never in the cards."

"You jump in and out of fantasy worlds to suit your argument."

"I just happen to feel more sentimental about the children I never had with you than the children I never had with her. I'm a romantic that way. So shoot me. Why did we get together, if it was all so unlikely?"

Louise considers the question for a moment.

"Because I was going through a dry spell," she says.

Tom is appalled.

"That's it?" he says.

"You asked why we got together, not why we stayed together. Did you have any long-term designs the night we met?"

"Well, yes. But the long-term became short-term pretty quickly."

"Because I was so easy, you mean?"

"Agreeable, I'd say, rather than easy."

"And then no plan?"

"Not no plan. Just . . . the same one."

"Isn't that how most couples get together? They want to end a dry spell, and then it all gets out of hand?"

"I suppose. Unless there's money involved. That woman with the huge breasts who married the billionaire . . . I don't know whether she was worried about a dry spell."

"And Jane says she knew she was going to marry Charlie the first time she saw him."

"And there are people who were friends for ages before they fell in love," Tom says.

"And arranged marriages."

"But still. As you point out. Plenty of people start with sex and go on from there."

"It's like, I don't know. Starting in a new job. One day follows another, and twenty years later you're still there. But you can't know on your first day."

"No. Otherwise you'd shoot yourself."

Louise gives him a look.

"If it was a boring job," he says.

"Do you remember anything about the first time we had sex?"

"What a question! Yes. Of course."

"Really? I can't."

"Neither can I."

"There was some disappointment, I think," Louise says.

"I'd hoped you'd forgotten all of it."

"That's why I wanted to give it another go. I didn't think it was fair to judge you on that one time."

"Ditto," Tom says defensively.

"What did I do wrong?"

"You were a bit . . . lackluster."

"Oh, it's all coming back to you now."

"I can't remember much. Just that you were, you know. Medium. Six out of ten. Six-point-five, maybe. Two-thirds, let's say. Me?"

"Well. It was basically a no-jump, wasn't it? Or a let. So I don't think I can give you a score."

"Can we not talk about this? It was nearly twenty years ago. We've gone on to better things."

"And back again," says Louise. "Like a pleasure cruiser."

"Perhaps that's the whole trajectory of married sex. Out round the rocks to look at the seals, and home."

"'Round the rocks'? 'To look at the seals'?"

"Or dolphins, or whatever."

"When were the dolphin years?"

"You know what I mean."

"Not really."

"I can remember some exotic spectaculars before the kids were born. Kitchen tables and so on."

"The kitchen table being the dolphin?"

"Yes," Tom says. "And the shower. And the garden."

"And didn't we do something . . . Oh. No. We didn't."

"What are you thinking of?"

"Nothing."

"It wasn't recently, was it? With your friend?"

"No. Of course not."

"Why 'of course not'?"

"Do you really want to go into this?" Louise says.

"Yes and no. I want to know and I'm terrified, all at the same time."

"It was just sex. No dolphins or seals."

"Or blindfolds."

"No! Why would you ask about blindfolds? Have you wanted me to wear a blindfold all these years?"

"Not . . . not really."

"Not really?"

"Not a blindfold as such."

"Can you draw this thing? If it's complicated? I'll try and knit one, if it helps."

Tom takes a pull on his drink.

"You must be bored," he says sadly.

"Are you?"

"You first."

"Now is hardly the time to ask me. I'm bored with nothing at all, that's for sure."

"What if I'd asked you a year ago?"

"You didn't," she says.

"So you won't answer hypothetical questions?"

"Why don't we just say it?"

"What?"

"We were both bored. It's become less and less important to us, and you packed it in, and then everything went wrong."

Tom doesn't say anything.

"Isn't that right?" says Louise.

"No."

"What have I got wrong?"

"I was never bored. But I did feel humiliated."

"Humiliated?"

"Because I knew. I knew you were bored. I could feel you were bored. There were . . . indications. And I got embarrassed to ask anymore, because I got knocked back so often."

Louise looks stricken.

"I'm sorry," she says. "I thought I knew where this conversation was going."

"Of course it's not your fault. Everything bounces back and forth between us. I'm boring, you get bored, I get more boring, you get more bored . . . Our sexual relationship is like a Newton's cradle."

"And even they stop, in the end," Louise says sadly.

Tom is genuinely surprised.

"Do they? I thought that was the whole point of them."

"You thought they went on forever?"

"Yes. I thought it was a perpetual-motion machine."

"So why aren't any still going?"

"I thought either because people got fed up with the clacking or they got fired and had to change offices."

"You know that perpetual-motion machines don't exist, don't you?" Louise says.

"No. I did not know that."

"If they did, all our energy problems would be solved forever."

"How can you run a car off a clacking executive toy?"

"It's not . . . We're getting sidetracked. But maybe that's what we expect marriage to be. A perpetual-motion machine that never runs out of energy. But we have kids, and a mortgage, your mother, my father, work, no work . . . How can one not be ground down by it?"

She starts to tear up a little bit.

"It's okay."

He reaches for her hand and squeezes it.

"I don't deserve that," she says.

"Why not?"

"Because I cheated on you and told you that I was bored in bed as an explanation."

"Yes," Tom says. "That plus my depression and unemployment."

"Oh. Yes. I'm a charmer. Being bored isn't the worst thing in the world."

"But life is long, and we're only just over halfway through it."

"I suspect it's only long if you're not enjoying it much."

"So there you are. I'm doing you a favor."

"Perpetual motion and relativity, all in one short conversation about our ongoing marital shambles," Louise says.

"Oh, yes. You need to be brainy to get out of being married to me."

She smiles while rummaging in her bag for a tissue. She blows her nose.

"I want to talk about the future today," Tom says.

"Good."

"Where it went."

"Oh."

"I can't see it. It used to be very clear to me. I was walking purposefully toward it. I was like one of those workers in a Soviet propaganda poster, pointing at it. It was shiny and bright, and full of . . . Well. I don't know what it was full of."

"Golden cornfields, factories, and tanks?"

"Yeah. My equivalent, anyway."

"Which was?"

"I can't remember."

"You can't remember the future?"

"Nope."

Outside the pub, as Tom and Louise cross the road, the old couple who see the counselor before them emerge from the front door.

"They've gone over their time."

"Who's been all the trouble, do you think? Seeing as they've been going on and off for years?"

They approach the couple. Tom nods as they pass. They are walking slowly, the man with some difficulty. The woman is tearful.

"Oh," says Louise.

"What?"

"I wonder if it's because he's not very well."

"Like, dying?"

"That may be what they're seeking help with now. Do you remember what she said? 'You've got lots of time. Lucky you.'"

"Oh, fuck. That's all we needed," says Tom. "She'll think we haven't got troubles, by comparison. She'll be impatient with us."

"But at least they'll make it through."

They have arrived at the front door of Kenyon's house.

"Is that the future? Making it through?"

"I'd settle for making it through," says Louise. "Making it through is the goal of every marriage, isn't it? I'm not sure there's anything else."

Tom rings the bell, and they wait in silence.

week nine

❦

PRISON SEX

tom is sitting in the pub, at their usual table, on his own, with the crossword (and a newspaper). He's cheerful—more energized, eyes sparkly. He is filling in the crossword with some ease—he writes in one answer, then another.

"Oh, get in."

He clenches his fist. Louise enters the pub and looks over to see whether Tom is there. She smiles when she sees him. She comes over and sits down.

"Hello."

"Well, hello," he says, with as much sleaze as he can manage.

Louise grins, almost embarrassed. Something is different in their interaction.

"How was your day?" says Tom.

"It was . . . It was fine. The, um . . . The night perked up the day no end."

"Same here."

"Thank you for asking. I mean it. I'm not being sarcastic, by the way. Really. Thank you for asking. I had a spring in my step for the first time in months."

"Well. Happy to oblige."

"I hope it didn't feel like an obligation," Louise says coyly.

"Of course not. (Even though, as you have pointed out several times, it really is, within marriage.)"

Louise takes a deep breath.

"Let's try and remain entirely positive," she says. "Last night was a real step forward, in our current circumstances, and we should just celebrate it."

"Agreed. I have been tweeting and instagramming all day."

Louise looks alarmed.

"Instagramming?" she says.

Tom rolls his eyes.

"Oh," she says.

"I note, however, that tweeting would have been fine. Did it feel . . . weird?"

"You first."

"Why should I answer my own question?"

"Okay," Louise says. "But first I want to ask you something."

"Unconnected to the weirdness?"

"Connected to the sex, only tangentially connected to the weirdness."

"Okay."

"Was it . . . Did you enjoy it?"

"Yes. Very much so. Oh, so now you answer the question in the light of that information."

"I didn't want to make a fool of myself."

"How would you do that?"

"Well," says Louise. "If you'd said, 'No, it was a complete waste of time' . . ."

"A complete waste of time? I could have been reading Proust, I suppose. But I could have done that instead of every sexual experience I've ever had. Or during, even."

"I just meant some phrase expressing dissatisfaction . . ."

"No dissatisfaction whatsoever."

"Anyway," Louise says. "So this is all in the context of what was to all intents and purposes a mutually fulfilling sexual experience."

"Well done. I think you've found the right language to describe our lovemaking to a panel of parliamentary ombudsmen. Carry on."

"It felt weird."

"It did, a bit."

"You agree?"

"Yes. It wasn't like marital sex at all."

"No. It was a bit like I'd imagine post-prison sex to be."

"Post-prison?" Tom says. "First of all, who's been in prison?"

"Well. You more than me."

"I don't think you can describe it comparatively. Either you've been in or you haven't."

"Well, we've both been in prison, sexually speaking, apart from my . . ."

"Mistakes."

"Yes. And you should know that my mistakes were not in any way . . . Well, they didn't commute the sentence, if you see what I mean."

"No," says Tom. "I don't."

"If the sexual prison sentence is defined by how much time you serve before . . . Well, before release . . ."

"I don't see how you can define prison as anything else, really."

"When you're in a sexual prison, you're talking about sexual re-lease."

Comprehension dawns on Tom's face.

"Ah." He's delighted. "There was no release of that kind?"

"No. That wasn't what it was about. And I didn't feel in the right frame of mind, anyway."

"Ha! Well, that puts a whole different complexion on things. If you don't mind me saying so, that's a real relief to me."

"I slept with someone else because I wasn't feeling very close to any adult human being. I was lonely, and I didn't feel wanted."

This sad confession doesn't check Tom's chirpiness.

"Still," he says. "No fireworks."

"No. No fireworks. Just warmth and solace."

Tom makes a face, to suggest that warmth and solace are of only marginal interest.

"This prison-sex thing, though . . . What would I have been in prison for?"

"Nothing bad," says Louise.

Tom is a little disappointed.

"It must have been something bad, by definition."

"Yeah, but tax evasion. Insider trading. That sort of thing."

"Those people are the pits. And also not terribly sexy."

"Neither are people covered in tattoos who've been lifting weights for fifteen years. I'd be scared to have sex with one of those."

"I also think you're unlikely to have married him in the first place."

"I could have met him on Tinder or one of those things."

"Well, again. Unlikely to have swiped whichever way you swipe."

He makes a face intended to convey a violent sex-starved convict, and then cuts to an impersonation of Louise on her phone, looking mildly intrigued and swiping.

"How do you know you swipe at all?"

"It's common knowledge."

"Not to me it's not," says Louise.

"Anyway, just to be clear: It was good, honest, unthreatening, tax-evader sex, not tattooed manslaughter sex."

"Yes. But actually, without all the, the shortcomings that might be implied by the prison sentence."

"What sort of shortcomings are implied by tax-evader sex?"

"Again, it's not the tax evasion that's significant. It's the release from prison. So, the obvious shortcomings."

"Well, I think I avoided those."

"You know you did."

"I thought I had. But good to have it confirmed."

They sip drinks and look around the pub. For the first time during their pre-counseling ritual, they have nothing to say to each other.

"But it wasn't . . . just sex to you, was it?" Louise says.

"How do you mean?"

"Without feelings."

"How would that work? You think I picked you up for a meaningless fling after we'd got our two children into bed?"

"No, but . . . I wondered whether I was just a body. It felt, I don't know. Like you'd somehow separated my bits from me."

"Well, that's the prison effect."

"I suppose so."

"But it was good sex."

"Yes," says Louise. "Really good sex. But sort of . . . unsettlingly good."

"So you're now saying we had the wrong kind of sex? I thought any kind of sex was the right kind of sex."

"Yes, that's what I thought before yesterday."

Tom lets out a weary sigh.

"I remember . . . It must have been a couple of years after the kids were born," he says, "and you were feeling fat and unattractive . . ."

"Thank you." She's being sarcastic.

116

"Oh, come on, Louise. I didn't think you were fat and unattractive! You thought you were fat and unattractive!"

"Go on."

"And you asked me, after we'd made love, whether I only wanted to because I loved you. Not because I fancied you."

"Yes. That was how I felt then. Ten years ago. And now I feel something different."

"And in those ten years, despite everything you of all people know about the decay of the human body, you've somehow become Kim Kardashian?"

"Meaning what, exactly?"

"Isn't it nice to be a sex object in your forties? And exactly what you wanted in your thirties? When you were feeling fat and unattractive?"

"Do you have to say the words over and over again?"

"You're not fat now. Nobody could say you were fat."

They both realize the omission at the same time. Louise is the first to react.

"But unattractive?"

"Or unattractive."

"You waited just that moment too long. And also, you more or less admitted that I was fat back then."

"Now I don't know what to say."

"Just say the right thing, and then you won't have to worry."

"How about this? All sex with you is the right kind of sex. You've never been fat. You've never been skinny. I've always been attracted to you."

Louise thinks about this. She can find no objection, so she moves on.

"You getting out of prison doesn't make me a . . . a sex object," she says. "It just means I was conveniently placed."

"I hate to be unromantic, but convenient placement is pretty much the definition of marital sex. I put my book down, look over to the other side of the bed, and there you are."

"That's different. Last night it felt as though I were a conveniently placed stranger."

"But . . . people pay a lot of money to turn their husbands into conveniently placed strangers!"

Louise wrinkles her nose up in distaste.

"Who do they pay?"

"I'm talking about sex therapy and so on. Isn't that what they say? Make it strange? And it worked!"

"It's not going to work for long, though."

Tom throws up his arms in mock despair.

"Right. I give up," he says. "We stopped making love because you were bored and I knew it. And then you weren't bored when we started again, but you didn't like the lack of boredom because it made you feel weird. And now you're lamenting the inevitable lack of weirdness if we do it more often."

"I can see that might be confusing. But I don't like you saying *if* we do it again."

"Don't you?"

"No. In an ideal world, I'd only want sex with you."

"Wow."

"Is that really worth a 'Wow'?"

"God, yes. I had no idea. That's quite romantic, for you."

"Really?" Louise says. "The 'ideal world' part is a pretty big get-out clause."

"Ah."

"Because, let's face it, this is not an ideal world."

"No. But do you mean the actual world or our world?"

"I wouldn't necessarily need the actual world to be ideal before committing to monogamy."

"Good to know. Anyway. The point is, you weren't saying as much as I thought."

Tom looks out of the window. The elderly lady who takes the earlier slot with the therapist is walking slowly across the road. Her husband isn't with her.

"Oh, shit," he says.

"What's happened?"

"She's on her own."

"Oh, dear. He probably just wasn't well enough to come."

"Let's hope. Otherwise . . ."

"Maybe it's nothing to do with his health. Maybe they split up. Maybe he told her where to get off."

"Or she's shagging around. That would be good."

"Why would it be good?" says Louise. "I would have thought you'd take a dim view of infidelity."

"I take a dim view of your infidelity. I don't mind hers."

"Because it means there's still fight?"

"Exactly. It shows you're alive, and uncertain. Nothing's fixed. I like that. Plus, she's someone I don't know and don't care about very much. That helps."

"But nothing's irreversible, isn't that the point?" says Louise. "You can still look around to see what's available, however old you are."

"Exactly."

"I think you should move back in."

week ten

❦

ANOTHER DRINK

om and Louise walk into the pub together and head toward the bar.

"We haven't arrived at the same time once in the last ten weeks," says Tom.

"It's an omen."

Tom asks for a pint of London Pride and a dry white.

"Aren't omens bad?"

"Don't they just predict change? Well, there you are. We arrive at the pub together for our last session."

Louise looks at him.

"Why is it our last session?" she says.

"I've moved back in. We've had sex twice in the last eight days. Sorted."

"First of all, when we started seeing Kenyon you hadn't even moved out. So you moving in just takes us back to where we started. And the sex . . ."

"Don't start on the sex. Leave it alone. We're having it. Don't knock it. It's my only accomplishment of the year."

"All I was going to say is that it should be there. We're married. We're not old. We should be having sex."

"And we are. We went because we stopped. Now we've started. Done. Tick. Let's move on."

They take their drinks and walk over to their usual table.

"But what happened to your feelings of humiliation?" Louise says.

"Gone. We had sex."

"What happened to your hurt and anger about my affair?"

"Ah, I've buried it deep. It will only reemerge as a physical illness, a heart attack, or cancer."

They sit down.

"And you think that's healthy?"

"Do I think heart disease and cancer are healthy? No, I do not."

"But the burying, which will result in cancer? Do you think that's healthy?"

"Yes, I do," Tom says sincerely. "In the short term."

"And what about the other things we've talked about in the sessions?"

"Like what?"

"Tom, in the last few weeks we've both aired more grievances than, than . . ."

"You'd be looking at some kind of peace process, I'd have thought. Middle East. Northern Ireland."

"I was trying to avoid the clichés."

"When it comes down to it, most peace processes are about one grievance. We have a thousand. So I don't know what the right analogy would be."

"Ours comes down to one, really," says Louise.

"Go on."

"We're married. Everything else is an offshoot. We wouldn't be arguing about, I don't know, my sister if we weren't married. You'd just say, 'How's your sister?'"

"If I even knew you had one. Indeed, if I even knew you."

"I'm presuming we'd be friends."

"Do you think we would?"

"In the right circumstances."

"Talk me through them."

"Don't be so rude," Louise says.

"Why is that rude?"

"Sarcastic, then."

"You were the one who said we'd only be friends 'in the right circumstances.' Why is it sarcastic to ask what those circumstances might be? I'd simply presumed that we'd be friends in all circumstances."

"You weren't presuming that at all. You were just trying to make me feel bad."

Tom thinks about this.

"You're right," he says. "That's depressing."

"Which bit?"

"You knew I was winding you up when I said I can't imagine us not being friends. In other words, I was suggesting the complete opposite is true. But husbands and wives don't have to be friends, do they?"

"I'd have thought so, yes. Let's say that on the night we met, we hadn't ended up going to bed together," Louise says. "Let's say we had an interesting and enjoyable conversation and then went our separate ways. What then?"

"What then what?"

"Would you have followed up?"

"Yes, of course."

"Why 'of course'?"

"Because I wanted to sleep with you."

"Sex is off the table."

"Why?"

"Because in the parallel universe I'm describing, we're not attracted to each other."

"Oh," Tom says. "Well, I wouldn't have spoken to you in the first place."

"You were that shallow?"

"It was a party. We were in our twenties. You have a good look round the room, and you think, *Well, I'll start there.* And you were where I started."

"How about this, then: We have a mutual friend who asks us round to dinner. We get on. The mutual friend asks us to dinner again. We get on again. The third time it happens, we exchange numbers and agree to go out for a drink."

"So sex is back on the table."

"No."

"I'm not following any of this."

"I'm talking about friendship. Could we have been friends if we hadn't slept together?"

"I can't see it."

"Thanks."

"The thing is, I didn't have any friends like you. I still don't have any friends like you. When I met you, you had no idea why anyone would shout 'Judas' at Bob Dylan."

"Now I even know the shouter's name."

This makes Tom happy.

"Do you?"

"Yes," says Louise. "Keith Butler. He lives in Toronto."

Tom is genuinely impressed.

"Wow."

"Sidetrack."

"I don't think I knew anyone who had a Biology O Level, let alone someone who would devote their life to the health problems of elderly people."

"You hardly knew anyone who cleaned their teeth."

"I cleaned mine," Tom says. "Still do."

"I know. But where are you going with Keith Butler and geron-tology?"

"Don't you see? They're what's so great about sex."

"Really? There's nothing else you can think of?"

"Forget about Keith Butler and old people. I'm talking about sexual attraction. Sometimes we want sex with people who don't belong in our particular . . . category."

"Especially so in your case," Louise says. "Otherwise you'd only have sex with slightly malodorous men with a bad pot habit who only see daylight during the festival season."

"What about Kim?"

"Or a slightly malodorous woman with a bad pot habit who only sees daylight during the festival season."

"Lots of people think she's sexy."

"'Sexy' in this case meaning 'owns a lot of old records.'"

Tom makes a face, as if to say, *Well, what else could "sexy" mean?*

"But you know what I'm saying," Tom says. "We wouldn't have been friends. But we slept together and found all sorts of things we had in common that we'd never have come across otherwise."

"For example?"

"Crosswords."

"That's one."

There is a pause.

"Kids."

"You can't put kids on the list," Louise says.

"Why not?"

"They weren't a shared interest before we had them."

"We both wanted them. If it had been dogs, and we'd ended up with a couple of cocker spaniels, you'd have allowed it."

"All right. Kids and crosswords."

"And I like the way you think. I've never met anyone who thinks like you."

"About what?"

Tom gestures vaguely.

"The world. Science. That sort of thing."

"This is nonsense."

"Yes, I'm afraid it is."

"You don't care how I think."

"Not really," says Tom cheerfully. "So we're not friends, is that the upshot?"

"It's not a helpful way of looking at things. We're married. It's different. We have created a whole life together despite everything. A language, a family. Some kind of understanding. An intimate knowledge of everything to do with the other person. What would you call all that?"

"Well. I know what Kenyon would call all that."

"I fear so."

"I suppose it is, though, isn't it?"

"I think it might be," Louise says.

"Huh."

"So why is that such an unsatisfactory answer?"

"I know what you mean."

"Do you?"

"I even think I know why."

"Go on."

"You won't be angry with me?" says Tom.

"No."

"Well, it's love, but without the feeling, if you know what I mean."

"Exactly!"

"Oh, phew."

"Love without the feeling!" says Louise with excitement. "That's it!"

"You don't need to be that enthusiastic."

"I mean, why are the kids always saying 'Love you!' 'Love you, Mum!' 'Love you, Dad!'?"

"I never said that to my parents."

"Well, there's a reason for that. But they say it all the time."

"I do think they love us. But deep down, maybe. Not on the surface, where cheap sentiment lives."

"So when they say it, it's cheap sentiment?"

"Means nothing."

"Do you think that's why we don't say 'I love you' to each other?" Louise says.

"I do, yes. We don't use the expression glibly. We save it for when it counts."

"Plus, we love without feeling."

"Perhaps we should practice saying it anyway. We know it wouldn't be glib with us. It would be a simple, factual recognition of the state that exists between us."

"I think that's a good idea."

Neither of them says anything.

"Let's put it on the list," says Tom.

"Might be a good thing to do with Kenyon."

"Absolutely."

"You know how you have to go to AA meetings even when you've given up drink?"

"Yes, of course. They have to keep saying they're alcoholics forever. 'My name's Tom, and I've been sober for ten years.' I'm not an alcoholic, by the way."

"That's for discussion another time. Well, I think we might be like that."

"Like what?"

"Sort of, 'Our names are Tom and Louise, and we are in a permanent marital crisis, even though we live together and have sex.'"

"I'm not seeing Kenyon forever."

"No. I wasn't saying that. But I think we should acknowledge that we have a flawed marriage. We live on a fault line, and the house might collapse at any moment."

"And there's nothing we can do about that? When we started, you said you wanted to rebuild the architecture of our entire marriage."

"I remember that," Louise says.

"But it can't be done."

"I wouldn't have thought so, no. Otherwise it wouldn't be our marriage anymore."

"No. But it might actually be somewhere we might want to live."

Louise spots the old couple emerge from Kenyon's house.

"Look! He's still with us!"

Tom grins.

"Oh, wow. That's made me feel quite hopeful about everything."

"Would you like another drink?"

Tom looks at her, astonished. It's as if Brigitte Bardot had offered him sex in 1963.

"Are you serious?"

"Yes. Let's get drunk."

"What about Kenyon?"

"I'll text saying that there has been a child emergency. You go and get the drinks."

Tom still cannot absorb his good fortune.

"I don't know what to say."

He stands up and heads for the bar, but then turns back to her.

"I do know what to say. I love you."

He doesn't mean it. Louise rolls her eyes and begins to look for Kenyon's phone number.

NICK HORNBY is the author of the bestselling novels
Funny Girl; *Juliet, Naked*; *Slam*; *A Long Way Down*;
How to Be Good; *High Fidelity*; and *About a Boy*;
and the memoir *Fever Pitch*. He is also the author
of *Songbook* (a finalist for a National Book Critics
Circle Award), *Shakespeare Wrote for Money*, and
The Polysyllabic Spree, and editor of the short story
collection *Speaking with the Angel*. A recipient of
the American Academy of Arts and Letters' E. M.
Forster Award and Oscar-nominated for his screen-
plays for *An Education* and *Brooklyn*, Hornby lives
in North London.